Frog's Riddle

& other
Draw-and-Tell
stories

Richard Thompson

Annick Press Ltd.
Toronto • New York

To the real Aubrey, Angela and Andrea

© 1990 Richard Thompson (text and drawings)
design and graphic realization by Monica Charny

Second printing, February 1994

Annick Press Ltd.

Annick Press gratefully acknowledges the support of the Canada
Council and the Ontario Arts Council.

Canadian Cataloguing in Publication Data

Thompson, Richard, 1951–
  Frogs riddle and other draw-and-tell stories

ISBN 1-55037-138-X

1. Reading (Elementary)—Language experience
approach. 2. Language arts (Elementary).
I. Title.

LB1573.33.T49 1990 372.4'14 C90-095294-6

Distributed in Canada by:
Firefly Books Ltd.
250 Sparks Ave.
Willowdale, ON M2H 2S4

Published in the U.S.A. by Annick Press (U.S.) Ltd.
Distributed in the U.S.A. by:
Firefly Books (U.S.) Inc.
P.O. Box 1325
Ellicott Station
Buffalo, New York 14205

Printed and bound by
Everbest, Hong Kong

Contents

FOREWORD

During Early Childhood Education training, my classmates and I spent time analyzing children's play activities and identifying the kinds of learning inherent in each activity.

At the playdough table—roll it out, smush it, make a ball, stick it together, make a snowman, pound it on the table, give a piece to Sally, make some cookies, make a pizza, "MY snake is blue. He is very fat. His name is Jerry. This is my dog, and this is my brother . . .". We were taught to observe in children gross and fine motor development, language development, development of social skills, intellectual and creative development. Dressing up, running and climbing, painting, colouring, cutting and pasting, playing with puzzles, building with blocks, reading and listening to stories, dancing, singing . . . all were learning and growing experiences. I concluded that the pursuits that were the most engaging for children were also the most powerful learning tools. I know the same principle applies at any age.

In the year and a half since the first *Draw-and-Tell* was published, I have visited hundreds of classes to read my books and tell stories. Repeatedly, the children in my audiences have confirmed my original hope—that for them, these stories are fun.

I have written the stories in this second collection for the same reason I wrote the first ones—because I enjoy writing and telling them and because I know that children have pleasure in listening to and telling them.

Teachers who have seen and used *Draw-and-Tell* have confirmed that these stories have been a useful tool in helping to develop and enhance language skills, in fostering imaginative thinking and in creating a positive attitude toward language learning.

So whether you are using these stories as teaching tools or "just for fun"—HAVE FUN!

Richard Thompson

A DRAW-AND-TELL WORKSHOP

One of the common reactions I get from teachers who have seen *Draw-and-Tell* is an enthusiastic, "I can hardly wait to get my students writing their own draw-and-tell stories!" What follows is a suggested sequence of activities leading toward that goal. You will want to adapt some parts, skip a step, perhaps, and add ideas of your own, knowing the needs of your students.

LEARNING THE STORY

Start with one of the stories at the beginning of the book, one that doesn't use extra devices such as flipping the drawing.
— Read the story.
— Draw the figure on a small piece of paper and try to relate key elements in the story to the parts of the drawing.
— Compare your drawing with the "map" that accompanies the story, noting missing elements.
— Repeat the last two steps until you have a feeling for the relationship between the story elements and the figure. Draw each section of the figure in a different-coloured pen to highlight exactly where each piece begins and ends.
— Try telling the story with the book close-at-hand for reference. With some draw-and-tell stories you are drawing all or most of the time you are talking. That is not the case with these stories. You will often find yourself telling long passages of the story without referring to the drawing at all.
— Practise a few times until you can tell the story without the book. Do not learn the story word for word—in fact, the story will be more effective if you have a good grasp of the structure of the story and can feel free to use your own words within that structure.
— Note the TELLING POINTS that follow each story. The TELLING POINTS are there to alert you to important story elements and to suggest ways to enhance your telling.
— Practise the story in the actual format that you will use when presenting it to an audience.

TELLING THE STORY

When you are story-telling with children who have had some previous exposure to draw-and-tell stories, you will want to remind them to "keep the secret". By establishing a "secret signal" before you start, you can allow the children the fun of guessing without disrupting the story. "There is a surprise in this story. If you guess the surprise, touch your nose once, like this. I will know that you know, and then it will be OUR secret!"
— Repeat the story another day. Even after they know the secret, children enjoy the story for it's own sake. It is partly through repeated telling that the children will begin to learn the story well enough to attempt a retelling of their own.
— Tell the story using a different, coloured marker for each step as you did when you were learning the story.
— Tell the story incorporating some of the variations suggested in the FURTHER ADVENTURES.

TELLING ON THEIR OWN

— Have the children work as a whole group to identify the key points of the story and map them on a completed drawing.

— Encourage the children to think in terms of the structure and pattern of the story. With that in mind, it is probably best not to provide the children with a copy of the story. Allow them to reconstruct the story from their knowledge of the structure and pattern and from their memory of your telling. With the MAP as a reference, have them work through the steps, outlined above, for learning the story.

— Encourage them to tell their version of the story—in partners, in small groups, to their class and other classes in the school. You might want to have the students work in pairs with one learning the figure and the other learning the story so they can present it as a team.

— Remind the students that during the presentations, they should try to remember to use a clear, audible voice and to face their audience when speaking. It takes a bit of practice to co-ordinate the drawing and speaking aspects of the story, but as much as possible, the teller should face the audience, not the easel.

— Keep in mind that the process is more important than the product. Any story is created anew with each teller. The version that you tell and the versions that your students tell again, will all be different from the story I had in mind when I wrote it. The figure may also look different from mine. That is what story-telling is all about.

— Encourage the students to retell the story with some of the variations suggested in the FURTHER ADVENTURES. When they have had a chance to try out a few of the stories in the book, your students may feel they are ready to try to work on stories of their own.

ADAPTING AN EXISTING DRAWING

— See the FURTHER ADVENTURES OF FROG'S RIDDLE (page 57) and the FURTHER ADVENTURES WITH THE LOCKED BOX (page 49) for some suggestions for adapting those stories.

— In THE PIZZA PEDALLER (page 81), how would it change the story if you were to add a flag for the bicycle, a basket on the front or a water bottle on the frame?

— There are several stories in *Draw-and-Tell*—UNCLE BOB, ALEXANDER, and THE PRINCESS AND THE CRITTER, that are particularly good as starting points for this exercise.

REWRITING THE STORY WITHIN THE EXISTING STRUCTURE

— Again, see the FURTHER ADVENTURES OF FROG'S RIDDLE (page 57) and the FURTHER ADVENTURES WITH THE LOCKED BOX (page 49).

— Make up a different "journey story" for the TIKI AND BUKO (page 17) figure. You might want to have the two friends travelling together right from the start.

— Make up a different story for THE HORN PLAYERS (page 25) figure. For example, Bob could be a paleontologist who sails in a boat to a far away land on an expedition to find evidence of the existence of a strange and heretofore unknown dinosaur.

BRAINSTORMING

— Draw simple abstract figures, different kinds of lines and geometric shapes. Work together to brainstorm a list of things each shape could be. For example, a circle might be a button, a coin, a small lake, a bowl, a cookie, a fingerprint, the path made by someone walking in a circle, a wheel, the sun, the moon, a planet, a sign or an eye.
— Turn the image and repeat the process. A tall, thin triangle that suggested a pine tree or a mountain might look more like an icicle, a pennant or an ice cream cone when you turn it the other way.

BRINGING THE ELEMENTS TOGETHER

— Using the collection of shapes and lines you have been working with, and the lists of suggestions that you generated in the last exercise, select several shapes and combine them into a story. Don't worry about coming up with a recognizable image.
— Take a piece of construction paper and rip it randomly into four or five odd-shaped pieces. Look at each piece and decide what it reminds you of. You might end up with a mountain, a boot, a porpoise and an apple. Put them together into a story.

SELECTING AN IMAGE

—Your image should be simple enough to be easily repeatable, but not so simple that you don't have any story-line. A map of North America might be a little too complex, for example. A drawing of an egg, on the other hand, doesn't give you much to work with.
— You may want to start with an existing image—a photo, a picture, a drawing or an illustration and work at simplifying and abstracting that image. Add and subtract details.
— Select an image that your audience will recognize. If they are going to be able to share in the surprise at the end, they need to know what the image is.
— Remember that symmetrical images and images with repetitive elements will be harder to make a story around. If you decide to finish with a picture of a centipede, you are going to have to think of fifty different things that the legs can represent in your story.

WRITING THE STORY

— For the first story, you may want to start with a simple "travel motif". The figure develops as the character moves from place to place.
— The story should work as a story. Ending up with a satisfying story is at least as important as ending up with a well-drawn figure.
— You will find that you have to modify your image to fit the story and rearrange parts of the story to fit the image. Keep checking as you make these changes. Does the image still look like what you had in mind? If you give the tiger square eyes, does it still look like a tiger? If you decide that the tiger's tail is going to be a rope, how does it fit into the story? Would it make more sense if it was a snake, a river or a twisted stick? Which option works best for your story?
— Any trick elements like flipping the drawing, covering part of it and cutting or folding the drawing should be integrated into the story.

HAVE FUN!

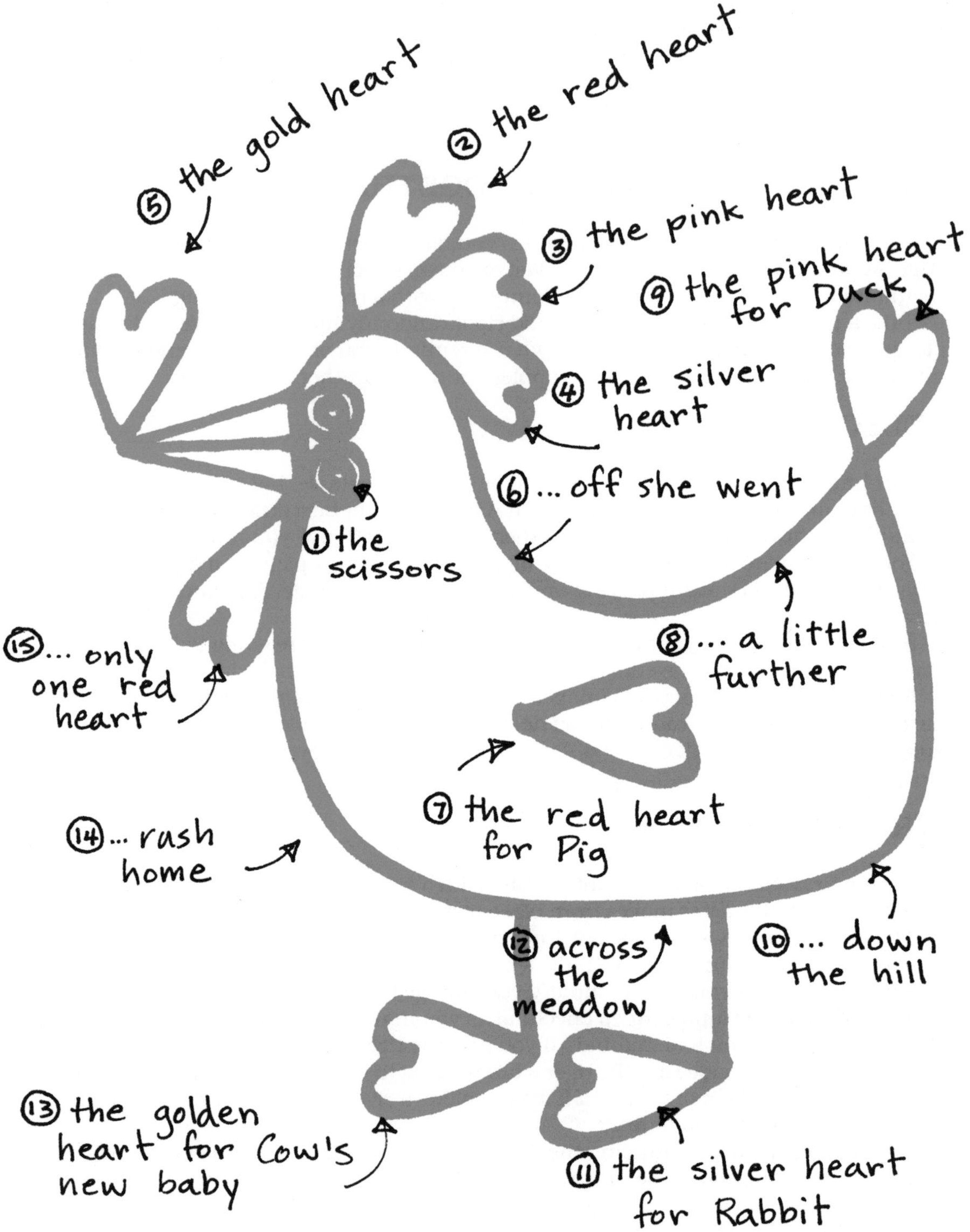

⑤ the gold heart

② the red heart

③ the pink heart

⑨ the pink heart for Duck

④ the silver heart

⑥ ...off she went

① the scissors

⑮ ...only one red heart

⑧ ...a little further

⑦ the red heart for Pig

⑭ ...rush home

⑫ across the meadow

⑩ ...down the hill

⑬ the golden heart for Cow's new baby

⑪ the silver heart for Rabbit

CLAUDETTE'S VALENTINES

Claudette borrowed a pair of scissors from her neighbour, and hurrying home, got right to work.

She took a piece of red paper and cut out a red heart . . .

She took a piece of pink paper and cut out a pink heart . . .

She took a piece of silver paper and cut out a silver heart . . .

. . . and finally she cut a gold heart from a piece of gold paper.

She bundled up these treasures and off she went. Right about here, she met Pig.

"Good day, Pig," she said. "Have you seen Ralph?"

"No," said Pig. "I've not seen Ralph at all."

"Oh, Pig," said Claudette. "Your tail is as straight as a stick. Are you sick?"

"A little snuffly," snuffled Pig.

"Well, Pig, you take this pretty red heart," said Claudette. "It might perk you up a bit." And she gave the red heart to Pig.

As Claudette walked on she thought that Pig's tail already looked a little curlier than it had.

A little further on, Claudette met Duck.

"Good day, Duck," she said. "Have you seen Ralph?"

"No," quacked Duck sadly. "I've not seen Ralph nor anyone else all day. And very lonely I'm feeling, too, Claudette, with my ducklings all grown up and flown away."

"Poor Duck," said Claudette. "You must come and have tea with me this afternoon. And in the meantime, this pretty pink Valentine will perk you up."

She gave Duck the pink Valentine.

Off Claudette went, down the hill toward the meadow where the grass grows tall.

She went up and knocked on the door of Rabbit's burrow.

"Good day, Rabbit," she said, when Rabbit stuck his head out. "Have you seen Ralph?"

"No," said Rabbit. "I've not seen Ralph. But then I haven't been out of my burrow all day. The basement is full of water and the plumber hasn't come. The children are squabbling. A gopher ran off with the last of the carrots! It's just been one of those days!"

"I'm sorry to hear that," said Claudette. "It isn't much, but perhaps it will take your mind off your troubles." And she handed Rabbit the silver heart.

"Thank you very much, Claudette," said Rabbit. "Oh, have you heard the news? Cow had a new baby this morning."

"Really?" said Claudette. "I will go and congratulate her right away."

She walked across the meadow to talk to Cow.

She admired the new baby.

"I don't have a present for him yet," she said, "but perhaps he would like this golden heart. I made it myself."

"That's very good of you," said Cow.

So Claudette gave Cow's new baby the golden heart.

"Oh, dear," she thought as she walked away. "I forgot to ask Cow if she'd seen Ralph. But . . . wait! I don't have any Valentines to give him now. I had best rush home and make him some more."

And that is what she did.

But she had only cut out one red heart when she looked out her window and saw Ralph coming toward her house.

He was carrying a golden heart in his beak, and if you guessed that that Valentine was for Claudette, you are right.

THE FURTHER ADVENTURES OF CLAUDETTE

1. Retell the story using coloured pens. If you can't find a gold and silver pen, perhaps you can find four different shades of red and pink to draw the hearts.

2. Retell the story using precut shapes for the hearts. Use sticky-back paper and stick each heart on in the appropriate place in the story.

3. Send yourself as a "storygram" to a special friend on Valentine's Day—go and visit and tell this story. You might want to use your name and your friend's name instead of Claudette and Ralph.

4. Design Valentine cards for Claudette's friends to send to her in return. What kind of card would a pig make?

5. Write a story describing Claudette and Ralph on a date. Where would two chickens go on a special outing? How would they get there? What would they eat? What would they talk about?

6. When you are having a terrible day, what makes you feel good? Make a list of "feel good" things and share the list with your friends.

7. Read *Alexander and the Terrible, Horrible, No Good, Very Bad Day* by Judith Viorst (Atheneum).

8. Claudette can tell that Pig is unwell because his tail isn't curly. Some folks say that you can tell a dog is sick if he doesn't have a cold nose. How can you tell if a goldfish is sick? An alligator under the weather? A llama has the flu? If you don't know, invent something. Share your ideas with the class.

9. Retell the story using different voices for each of the characters that Claudette meets.

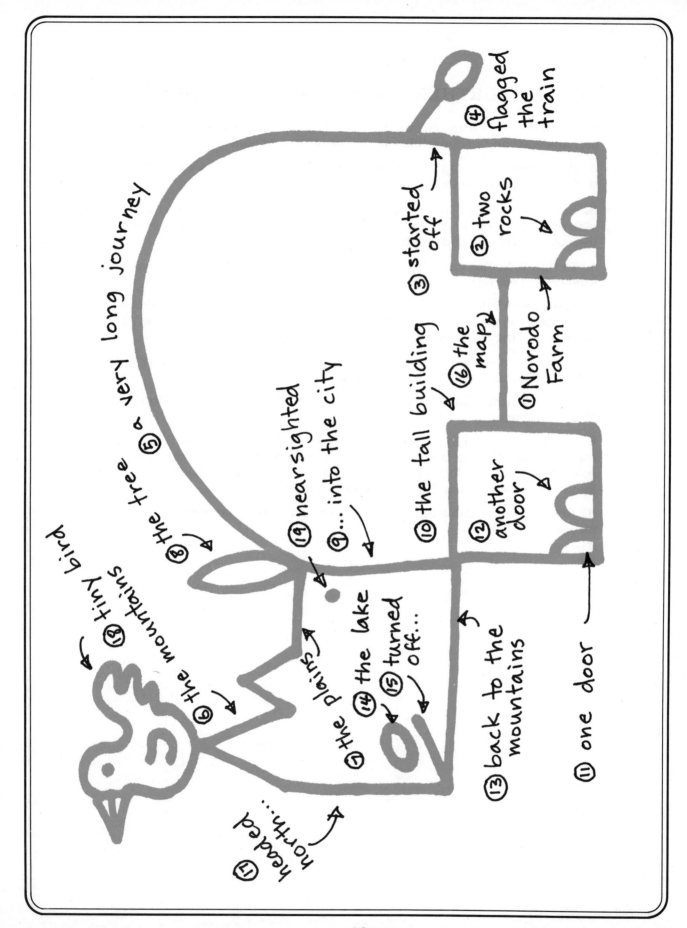

16

TIKI AND BUKO

Tiki's fondest wish was to be a train driver. Buko's fondest wish was to be able to see just a bit better—so he didn't keep running into rocks and trees. And it is because of those two wishes that you will always see Tiki and Buko together today.

When this story began, Buko lived on Norodo Farm. [*Here . . .*]

One day he was running along and BONK!—he ran into a rock. A few minutes later—BONK!—he ran into another rock. He decided then and there that he had finally run into one rock too many. He would go to the city and get himself some eyeglasses.

Early the next morning, he caught the train and started off on his journey.

Mr. and Mrs. Whirtle flagged the train a short time later and the train stopped to pick them up.

Buko was happy to have company,
because it was a very long trip.

Meanwhile, Tiki who lived in the mountains [*here*], was saying to herself: "It is all very fine to wish to be a train driver, but, if I really mean to be one, I will have to go and get a job with the train company."

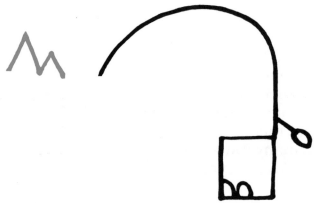

So she left her home in the mountains, trekked across the plain, and made herself comfortable in a tall tree near the tracks to wait for the train.

With Tiki on board, the train continued on into the city.

Buko got off the train as soon as it stopped and went straight to a tall building in the middle of the city. He went in one door [*here*] and took the elevator to the sixth floor where the optometrist had his office.

The optometrist quickly confirmed that Buko did need glasses and offered to sell him a pair for one hundred dollars. Unhappily, Buko had no money—not even enough to take the train back to Noroda Farm. He left the office building and sat in the park wondering what he should do next.

Meanwhile, Tiki had gone to the same office building. She had gone in another door [*here*] and had taken the elevator to the ninth floor to see the president of the railway company. The president of the railway company told her—none too politely—that she was much too small to be a train driver.

As Buko sat in the park thinking, Tiki set off to walk back to the mountains. She told herself that if they wouldn't let her drive the train, she wouldn't ride it either.

When night fell, Tiki found herself near a small lake. She turned off the main road to look for a place to sleep on the shores of the lake.

When night fell, Mr. and Mrs. Whirtle found Buko in the park. They listened to his sad story and drew him a map showing him how he could travel cross-country, back to the farm.

Buko set off at once, but, because of his poor eyesight, he became confused and ended up following in Tiki's footsteps on the road that led to the mountains.

Buko thundered along at a brisk run, determined to be home by morning.

Just as the sun was coming up, he heard a small voice cry out: "Stop! Stop! You'll run over me, you galumphing fool!"

Buko couldn't see who was calling, but he stopped instantly—that close to Tiki.

Poor Tiki, who was just waking up, was very frightened.

When Buko realized what had happened, he offered to make amends by giving Tiki a ride home.

With Tiki riding and Buko thundering along like a locomotive, they headed north toward the mountains.

"You know, Buko," said Tiki some time later, "riding up here is very much like I imagine driving a train would be."

"And with you up there saying Go right! Go left! —" said Buko, "I haven't run into a rock or tree all morning."

They both agreed that it was a very good arrangement. And they have been inseparable ever since.

So, if you are ever in Africa and you spot a tiny bird riding on the horn of a nearsighted rhinoceros . . .

. . . it is very likely Tiki and Buko that you are seeing.

THE FURTHER ADVENTURES OF TIKI AND BUKO

1. Tiki and Buko have what is known as a "symbiotic relationship"—they are very different from each other, but they live together and affect each other's lives. On your own or as a class try to think of other symbiotic relationships in nature or in human society.

2. The rhinoceros is an endangered species. Write away to: WORLD WILDLIFE FUND CANADA, 60 St. Clair Ave. East, Suite 201, Toronto, Ontario M4T 1N5 for information on endangered species in Canada and to find out what you can do to help.

3. Do some research to find out what qualifications and training a person would need to become a train driver. Report back to the class.

4. There is a bird that perches on a rhinoceros' back and eats ticks and other insects from amongst the folds of the animal's skin. Find out more about this bird and report to the class.

5. Draw a picture and/or write a description of what Buko would have seen from the train window—if he had been able to see better.

6. Using clay or baker's clay, make a three-dimensional map of the part of the world where Tiki and Buko travelled.

7. Read *Who Wants To Buy a Cheap Rhinoceros?* by Shel Silverstein (Collier).

8. Design an eye chart that an optometrist might use to test a rhinoceros' eyes. Can the rhinoceros read?

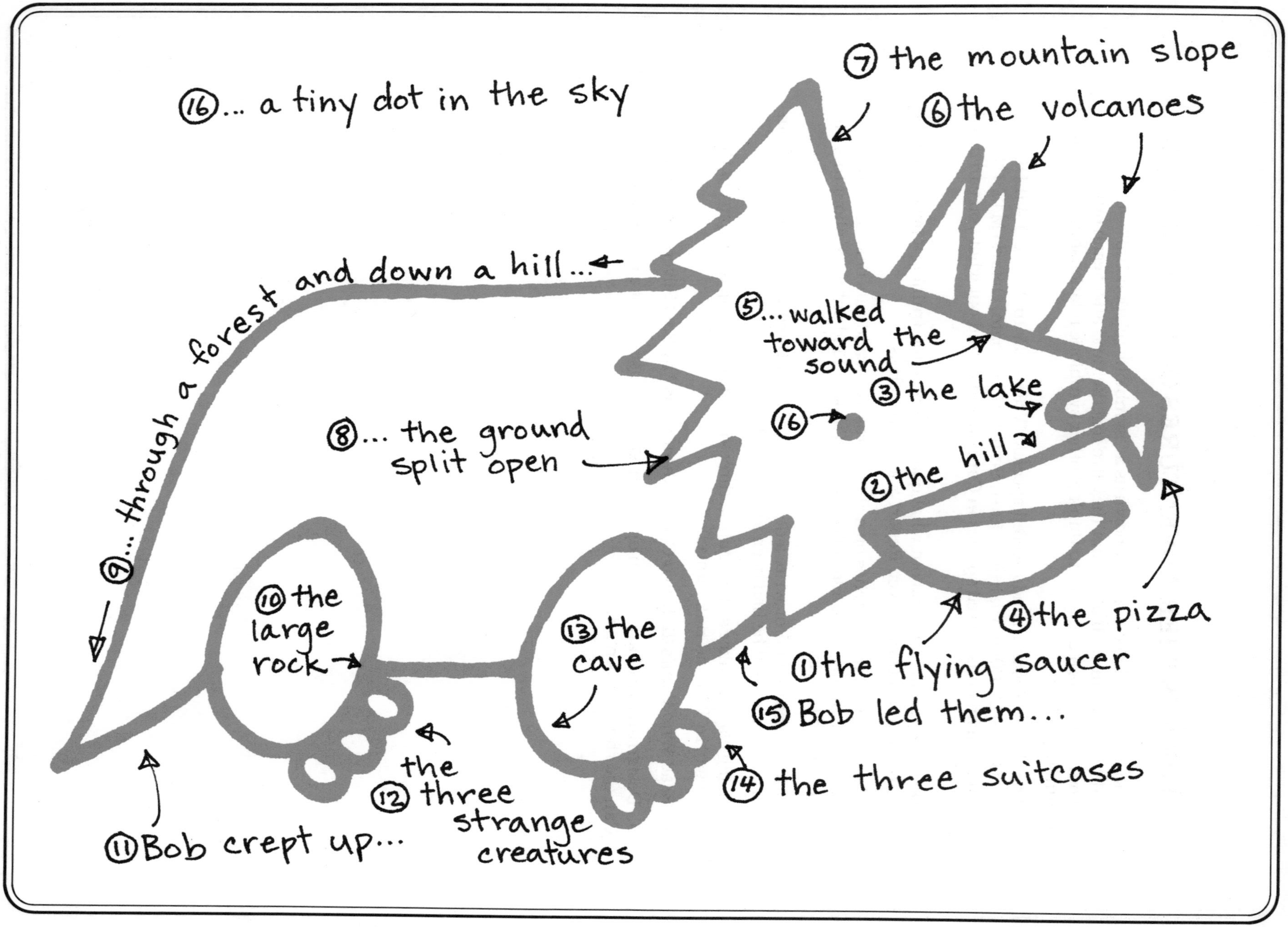
⑯... a tiny dot in the sky
⑦ the mountain slope
⑥ the volcanoes
⑨... through a forest and down a hill...
⑤... walked toward the sound
③ the lake
⑯
⑧... the ground split open
② the hill
④ the pizza
① the flying saucer
⑮ Bob led them...
⑩ the large rock
⑬ the cave
⑭ the three suitcases
⑫ the three strange creatures
⑪ Bob crept up...

THE HORN PLAYERS

Bob was an intergallactic talent scout from the planet Arpeggio. You've probably heard of SONJA AND THE SOLAR FLARES? THE SUPER NOVAS? THE BLACK HOLES? Bob discovered them all.

Well, one afternoon Bob was skimming along in his flying saucer when he spotted a pretty green and blue planet below and just to the left. It looked like a pleasant spot for a picnic, so he landed his saucer [*here*] . . .

. . . and got out. He walked up a little hill, sat down in a cool spot by a lake and began munching on a piece of cold pizza.

Faintly, from far away, he heard music. He stood up. He listened.

And then as if drawn by a magnet, he walked toward the haunting sound.

"It's definitely horns of some kind," he said to himself. "But what kind?"

On and on he walked.

"Trumpets? No, not trumpets. Trombones? Tubas? Whatever they're playing, it's beautiful."

He walked past three smouldering volcanoes.

"French horns? Cornets? What kind of music is this?"

He walked up a steep mountain slope and stood at the top listening, listening. The music was much louder now, but he still couldn't think what kind of horn it was that he was hearing.

Suddenly, the earth began to tremble. The music was drowned out by a horrendous cracking sound, and the ground split open right at Bob's feet—an earthquake!

Bob's first thought was to run back to his saucer and fly away. But when the earth was quiet again, he heard the music once more, and he knew he had to go on.

He walked through a forest and down a long hill deep into the swamp, drawn on and on by the music of the horns.

The music was very loud now. Bob looked around. There behind him was . . .

. . .a large rock.
Quietly, Bob crept up to the rock.

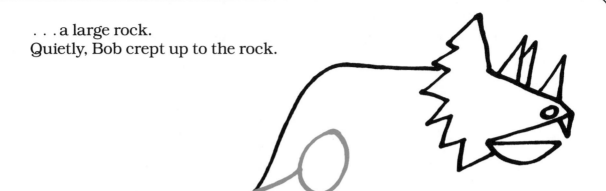

He looked over the rock. On the other side were three of the strangest creatures that Bob had ever seen. Each of them had three horns, and from those nine horns was coming the most exquisite music that Bob had ever heard.

Suddenly, one of the creatures spotted Bob. The music stopped. Quickly Bob scrambled over the rock.

"You guys are wonderful!" he cried. "You've got to come back to Arpeggio with me. You'll be famous! You'll be rich!"

The three creatures huddled together and talked.

Then, with a grunt, one of the creatures headed off into the swamp. The other two followed, and Bob ran along behind.

They came to a cave . . .

. . .where the three creatures began packing three suitcases.

"You're coming with me?" cried Bob. "You're really coming!"

The creatures finished packing and stood there waiting patiently for Bob to lead them to the flying saucer.

"What are we waiting for, guys? Let's go!"

Bob led the three creatures to his spaceship and off they flew.

Soon the flying saucer with Bob and the three horn players was no more than a tiny dot in the sky. And then it was gone.

As you probably guessed, those three creatures were three triceratopses. In fact, they were the last three triceratopses on Earth. That is why triceratopses are extinct. And that is kind of sad, because it means that you and I will never hear the beautiful music that a triceratops makes when it plays on its horns.

THE FURTHER ADVENTURES OF THE HORN PLAYERS

1. With some friends write a musical piece for triceratops, horns and kazoos. Perform it for the class.

2. Experiment with ways of making different "horn" sounds with your voice and use those sounds in the story. Invite your audience to join you in the music-making parts of the story.

3. Experiment with different "spaceship" sounds and use them in your story.

4. Imagine a triceratops dancing. Try out some triceratops' dances and put one in the story in the part where the three creatures are dancing around.

5. Think of dangers, other than the earthquake, that Bob might encounter in his search for the horn players. Put them into the story—perhaps in the part where Bob is going up past the volcanoes or in the part where he is going down through the forest.

6. Design a playbill for an evening's entertainment on Arpeggio. What other acts might be on the program in addition to the triceratops trio?

7. Read *Dinosaur Dreams* by Kerry Westell (Annick Press).

8. Learn and tell the story *William and Warble* from *Draw-and-Tell* by Richard Thompson (Annick Press).

9. Triceratopses couldn't really play music on their horns. But there was a kind of dinosaur that scientists believe might have been able to make honking sounds with the large crest on its head. Find out about this dinosaur and report to the class.

10. Make a list of all the great acts that Bob discovered and write a brief description of what the actors and actresses did during their performances.

11. What is a volcano? Use the reference book in the classroom or library for more information and for a picture. What types of volcanoes are there?

12. Where are SONJA AND SOLAR FLARES today? Write a piece for an inter-gallactic entertainment magazine. Or maybe you would rather chronicle the careers of the SUPER NOVAS or THE BLACK HOLES . . .

13. This story presents one theory to account for the extinction of the dinosaurs. Do some research and find out some other theories that scientists have to explain the disappearance of these creatures.

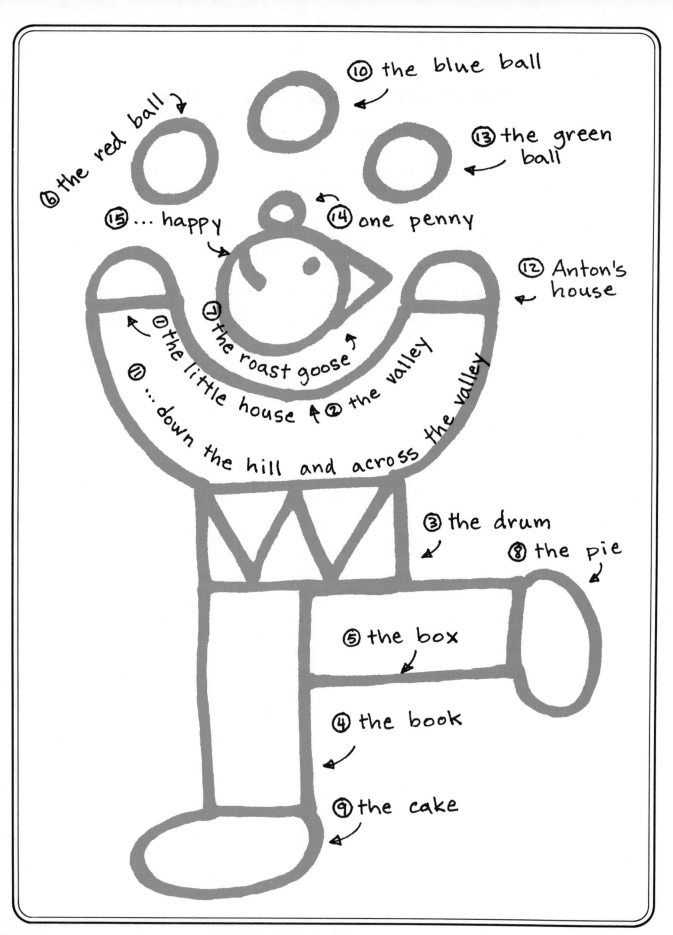

WILLY'S GIFT

Once a year Willy came to visit Simon and his family. Once a year he came to the little house that overlooked the green valley of the Tyne. Once a year he came with his bundle of gifts for the family.

One year he brought a drum for Tim . . .

. . . and a book for father.

For mother, he brought a beautifully crafted box.

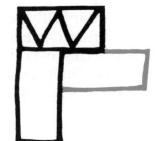

And for Simon, he brought a ball. A simple red ball. Simon was disappointed; he was too old to play with a ball. But he thanked Willy and joined with the others in celebrating the happy occasion.

For supper that night there was roast goose with . . .

. . . pie AND cake for dessert.

After dinner there was dancing and singing. And then, late in the evening, the family gathered in front of the fire to hear Willy tell of all the adventures he had had since the last time he had visited.

Listening to the stories in the warm glow of the fire, Simon fell asleep.

The next morning, when it was time for Willy to leave, he gave Simon a second ball, a blue one.

"This ball and the red one are only part of my gift to you," he said to Simon. "My friend, Anton, holds the other part. When you are old enough, you may come with me to Anton's house, and he will give it to you."

"But I am old enough now!" Simon declared. "May I go, Mother? Father?"

Simon's mother and father agreed, and Simon set off with Willy.

Down the hill they went, and across the valley . . .

. . . to the house of Willy's friend, Anton.

Anton gave Simon a third ball—a green one.

"But that is not all," said Willy.

"We will stay with Anton, Simon, and he will teach you the magic of the coloured balls."

So Simon stayed and watched and listened and practised until he, too, found the magic in the coloured balls.

And if you chance to meet him some day—on the street or at the fair, perhaps—for one penny he will be happy to show you Willy's gift.

THE FURTHER ADVENTURES OF WILLY'S GIFT

1. Retell the story using coloured pens.

2. Read *Juggling For the Complete Klutz* by John Cassidy and B.C. Rimbeaux (Klutz Press). *The Instant Juggling Book* by Bob Woodburn (Rethink Inc.) features easy beginner instructions as well as 40 tricks for the more experienced juggler.

3. You are Uncle Willy. Write an account of your travels in the year that has past since you last saw Simon and his family. Share it with your "family".

4. Willy has been coming to visit every year since Simon can remember. Make a list of all the gifts he has brought over the years for members of the family. Tell where each gift came from and anything that is unusual or noteworthy about that gift.

5. In times past it was common for young men and women to live and work with a master and learn a trade or skill. What master—past or present—would you choose to be apprenticed to? Why? What three things would you hope to learn from that teacher? Share your ideas with the class.

6. Visit your library or video store for a video on how to juggle.

7. Retell the story using precut shapes for the balls and parts of the gifts. Cut the shapes out beforehand from sticky-back paper and stick them on at the appropriate point in the story.

8. Simon comes home and tells his family that he wants to be a juggler and a clown. How do they react? Would Tim react differently than Simon's mother and father? How would your parents react if you told them you were going to join the circus? Discuss.

9. You can make this into a Christmas story or a birthday story simply by having Willy visit once a year either at Christmas time or on Simon's birthday.

TREE MITES

Peter was a city fellow. But he got fed up with the hurly-burly and decided to move out to the bush for a bit of peace and quiet. He bought himself thirty acres out near Summit Lake.

He built a tidy little cabin a quarter of a mile or so north of the lake—about half way up toward Rocky Knob. Come to think of it, it was probably about as close to Sugar Lump as it was to Rocky Knob . . .

Anyway, he'd been living there for a couple of weeks, when one day he went outside and saw that some varmint had been poaching his timber! The evidence was right there for anybody to see—a grandaddy old spruce tree lying flat on the ground!

Peter was determined to find out who'd been chopping down his trees, and he figured if anyone around would have a line on the culprit it would be Artie Little. So he headed down along the lake and up the trail . . .

. . . to Artie's place.

"Well," Artie said, after he'd heard all the facts, "seems you've got tree mites, Pete."

Peter looked worried.

"They've been known to clear cut a mountainside in less than a week—every tree gnawed to the stump. You got a log cabin? Too bad! Once they run out of standing timber, those tree mites as likely as not will start in on the cabin."

Peter looked more worried.

"But you can scare them off. You've got to go up on a high bit of ground. Okay? Then you sit down cross-legged on the ground— that's right! Hook one finger in the corner of your mouth like this, and then another finger in the other corner like this. Good! Now start in flapping your elbows up and down and hollering: "Thrrrrrrrr . . . . . .!

That'll scare them off."

So Peter took the shortest path . . .

. . . straight over to Tea Pot Mountain. He
climbed right to the top of the mountain
and he did just what Artie told him.

He sat down on the ground, hooked one
finger in the corner of his mouth, hooked
another finger in the other corner of his
mouth, started flapping . . . and:
"Thrrrrrr . . . . . . !"

He kept it up for a whole hour!

He was feeling pretty happy as he headed
down along the lake and back up to his
cabin.

But then he saw that the tree mites had
been at it again. They had taken down three
saplings out behind the cabin.

Peter didn't hang around. He marched right up to the top of Rocky Knob.

He sat down on the ground, hooked one finger . . . hooked the other finger . . . got his elbows flapping and: "Thrrrrrr . . . . . . !"

He kept at it for two hours this time.

He was sure he'd cleared out any tree mites between here and Chetwyn, but as he was heading back to his cabin, he saw a spot on the north meadow where the grass was all trampled down. And not far off there was another spot just the same.

"Tree mite beds!" Peter figured.

So just to be double sure, he hiked up
Sugar Lump and tried one more time.

He sat down cross-legged, hooked a finger
in the corner of his mouth . . . hooked
another finger in the other corner of his
mouth . . . elbows flapping:
"Trrrrrr . . . ."

He kept it up until almost dark!

Peter headed down again to his cabin, but
as soon as he got within sight of the place,
he saw that three more trees were down.

He shook his head, and he said, "I give up! Let the blasted tree mites have the place!"

He just walked away, and no one ever saw him around here again.

Artie felt pretty bad about playing a trick on Peter, but I said, "Heck, Artie! Even a city fellow like him should have known that there's no such thing as tree mites!"

I bet YOU know what was chopping down Peter's trees . . .

That's right—a beaver!

TELLING POINTS

1. Remember to start the figure well to the left so you have room for the tail and the stump.

2. Encourage your audience to join in with the "tree mite scaring" when it comes up in the story. Kids are usually sitting down cross-legged to listen in the first place, so they are already doing the first step. As you begin to explain how it's done, look at someone who is already starting to follow your lead and say, "That's right! I see you've done this before!" Others will join in.

3. You don't need to say the part about the elbows if you are doing it—they'll get the idea.

4. The "trrrrr . . ." sound is made by vibrating the tongue against the top of the mouth. Any silly sound will do, though.

THE FURTHER ADVENTURES OF THE TREE MITES

1. How would you scare a tree mite! Make up your own "tree mite scaring call" and use it in the story.

2. *The Mare's Egg* is another story in which a person is tricked because of his innocence of the ways of the country. There are many variations of the story. Find one and share it with the class.

3. Draw a picture of a tree mite.

4. Write a "research paper" on tree mites. Report on such things as what tree mites eat, how many young they have and how they care for them, how tree mite babies are born, what tree mites do in the winter, what tree mites sound like, their sleeping habits, how big they are . . .

5. A bunch of cows is a herd, a bunch of geese is a flock. What is a bunch of tree mites called? On your own or in a group make up a list of possible words that might mean "a bunch of tree mites".

6. Find out some interesting facts about beavers and share them with the class. The beaver has featured prominently in Canada's history. Find out how and why and report to the class.

7. On your own or in a group make a list of as many different kinds of trees as you can think of or find in books.

8. Using clay or baker's clay construct a three dimensional map of the area around Summit Lake. Add details that aren't in the story.

9. Do you think "tree mites" might have been Artie's way of pronouncing "termites"? Find out some things about termites and report them to the class. Could termites actually chop down a tree? How would you go about getting rid of termites?

10. Would you prefer to live in the country or the city? On your own or as a class, make up a list of the plus and minus aspects of each.

① two doughnuts
② the box
③ ... fell in
④ the river
⑤ ... jumped in
⑥ the sailboat
⑦ the rope
⑧ the tree
⑨ the hill
⑩ the school
⑪ Marc's house
⑫ ... down the hill
⑬ Clinton's house

44

THE LOCKED BOX

Clinton got out of his sopping wet clothes and put on some dry ones. Then he went into the kitchen and got a snack for himself and his friend, Marc—a chocolate covered doughnut for himself and one with sprinkles for his friend.

"Have you figured out how to open it yet?" he asked his friend. Marc was sitting at the table looking at a metal box. The box was locked and Marc was trying to figure out the combination of six numbers that they needed to open the lock.

"Not yet," he said. "Tell me the story again . . ."

"Okay," said Clinton. "I was walking along and I found this box . . ."

Marc drew a picture of the box.

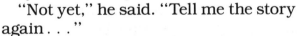

"I headed home and was walking across the bridge when I dropped the box. It sailed downnnnnnnnnn . . . and landed— SPLASH!—in the river. It started to float away on the current."

"Well, I wasn't about to lose my treasure. I jumped into the water and swam downstream after the box. I finally caught up with it about here."

"So you got the box and you swam to shore," said Marc.

"No," said Clinton, "Remember—a sailboat came along. They threw me a rope and pulled me aboard."

"They put me ashore, I dumped the water out of my shoes and started up the hill. That's when Muller's dog took off after me."

"And you got away from him by climbing up the big tree at the top of the hill?" questioned Marc.

"That's right," said Clinton. "But when the dog went away, and I climbed down from the tree, three big kids tried to take the box away from me. I got away from them by climbing the fence at the school, and that's where I met you."

"We came back to my house," said Marc. "You borrowed my sister's bike and we rode down the hill . . ."

. . . to your place. And here we are. AND I think I have figured out the numbers we need to open this box."

"You have!" said Clinton. "What are they?"

Do you know? That's right—8, 7, 3, 4, 5, 2.

They dialed those numbers on the lock, and the box popped open. Inside was—A SMALLER LOCKED BOX. And *you* will have to write the story of how Clinton and Marc got that box open.

TELLING POINTS

1. I have drawn the numbers on one line, but don't worry if you run out of room and have to put one or more letters below the others.

FURTHER ADVENTURES WITH THE LOCKED BOX

1. Imagine what might be in the small box. Make a list of possibilities.

2. Working alone or with a group choose a number from 0—9 and draw the number in as many different ways as you can. Make up a "mini-story" about each of your drawings. For example:

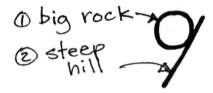 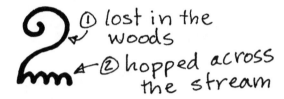

Share your ideas.

3. Replace one of the numbers in *The Locked Box* with one of your numbers and see how it changes the story.

4. Put two or more of the number ideas from FURTHER ADVENTURES #2 together into a longer story.

5. Add a number or two to the original *The Locked Box* and make a longer story about a box with a lock on it with seven, eight or nine numbers in the combination.

6. Find other stories with puzzles in them in *Stories to Solve—Folktales From Around the World* retold by George Shannon (Greenwillow).

7. For more fun with numbers read *It's All Done With Numbers* by Rose Wyler and Gerald Ames (Doubleday and Co.).

8. Write the "prequel" to this story. How did the box come to be lost? To whom does it really belong?

9. Tell the story as a duet, one person taking the role of Clinton, the other Marc. Tell the parts alternately, Clinton telling Marc what happened to him—"I found this box, see . . ." and Marc reiterating parts of the story—". . . and then you fell in the river, right?"

FROG'S RIDDLE

NOTE: For this story, besides a surface to draw on and something to draw with, you'll need a piece of black paper wide enough to cover the top half of the drawing—this is the dark. Have the paper at hand with pieces of tape on the upper corners ready to fix it in place over the drawing.

This is a story about a girl named Aubrey and her two sisters, Andrea and Angela. As soon as I draw you a picture of Aubrey you will be able to guess what kind of girl she was . . .

One day Aubrey caught a frog down by the river.

"You're not going to chop me up and make a potion are you, lady?" whimpered the frog. "Look, I'll make you a deal. You see if you can guess my name. If you can guess correctly by the time it gets dark, I'll give you three bags of gold AND you can chop me up. But if you don't guess, you gotta let me go. Okay?"

Now, Aubrey had no intention of chopping up the frog, but she liked the idea of getting three bags of gold, so she agreed.

"Bob? Arthur? Merlin? Fred? Brian? Alex? Charles?"

Aubrey guessed and guessed and guessed again, but "No . . . no . . . sorry . . . nope . . . no . . . nay . . . uhn . . . uhn . . ."

Finally, she stuffed the frog in her pocket, got on her broom and flew off toward the north. She flew over high mountains to . . .

. . . her sister, Andrea's house.

Andrea looked exactly like Aubrey except that she had curly hair instead of straight.

Aubrey told her about the deal. Andrea didn't waste any time guessing. Instead, she mixed up a gooey black potion in a stone bowl.

She dipped her finger in the potion and dobbed a black 'X' on Aubrey's forehead.

"The first name you think of when you close your eyes will be the frog's name," she said.

"Max!" declared Aubrey.

"Nope," said the frog.

"Angela will know," said Aubrey. Andrea agreed. The two of them jumped on their brooms, and headed north.

Now, Angela looked exactly like her sisters
except that she had kinky hair instead of
curly hair or straight.

She was just finishing her dinner when
her two sisters arrived.

She insisted that her sisters sit down and
help her finish the rest of her raspberry pie
before she would even listen to their story.

Finally, the pie was finished, and she
listened.

"Nothing could be easier," she said.
"We'll go up to the tower as soon as I've
finished my tea."

"Please hurry," said Aubrey. "It's almost
dark."

Tea finished, Angela led her sisters to the tower.

Up the stairs they went . . .

. . . to Angela's secret library.

Angela took a big book off the shelf.

"This is my book of names," she said. "Now, I'll just cross my toes and open the book. And the first name I see will be this frog's name. It's as easy as that!"

She crossed her toes and opened the book. She looked. She smiled.

"Dan!" she declared. "Your name is Dan!"

"Nope!"

"No?" said Angela. "Well, I guess we'll just have to go through the book one name at a time. We'll find it."

"Hurry," said Aubrey.

"Abigail. No? Abernathy. No? Able? No . . ."

Angela worked her way through the A's and B's.

Darkness began to fall.

[*Lower a piece of black paper slowly over the drawing as far as the dotted line.*]

She worked her way up to the J's.

Darkness came down, and down.

She tried a few M's: "Mike, Morgan, Melvin, Mort, Mitchell . . ."

She had just finished the R's, when the frog piped up, "Sorry, ladies. You lose."

The three sisters looked out the window at the darkness all around.

"Gotta go," said the frog. And . . . hop! hop! . . . he disappeared out the door.

"There goes our three bags of gold," said Aubrey sadly.

"He probably didn't even have a name," said Angela, shutting her book.

"If we couldn't guess it," declared Andrea, "then there's nobody who could."

But Angela was wrong. The frog did have a name. Can you guess what it was?

ALTERNATE ENDING . . .

"Gotta go," said the frog. He jumped out the window, dowwwwwn to the ground, and hopped away into the forest. "There goes our three bags of gold," said Aubrey sadly.

"He probably didn't even have a name," said Angela, shutting her book.

"If we couldn't guess it," declared Andrea, "then there's nobody who could."

But Angela was wrong. The frog did have a name. Can you guess what it was?

TELLING POINTS

1. When you start the story: ". . . you will be able to guess what kind of girl she was . . .", pause and give your audience time to guess.

2. You need to have a sheet of black paper ready for "the night". The paper needs to be large enough to cover the top two names. Have pieces of tape already in place on the corners so you can quickly tape it to the drawing when "night has fallen". Slowly lower the paper as the sisters make their final guesses.

3. You can use any three names for the sisters as long as they start with the letter "A". Whatever names you use, though, you will want to devise a way of remembering which name goes where in the story. For instance, I always start with Aubrey because it is different from the other two, and I always put Angela last because Angela sounds like "angel" and angels go at the top (nearest to heaven).

4. You might want to elicit names from your audience to help the sisters guess. If you do and someone says "SAM!" you have two options: one: pretend you didn't hear that person or two: be prepared to use the alternate ending or another alternate ending of your own creation. Also see FURTHER ADVENTURES #2.

5. If you want to make sure your audience knows where the story is going you may want to have Andrea say: "The name is "M", "A", "X"—Max!"—pointing to each letter as you say it.

THE FURTHER ADVENTURES OF FROG'S RIDDLE

1. What might go into the potion that Andrea makes? Think of some things and add that to your story. You might want to get your audience to suggest things to mix in.

2. Change "Max" or "Dan" to another three letter name with an "A" in the middle—Pat or Pam or Sal or Ray or Hal perhaps. How can you change the story to work in these new shapes?

3. If you were a witch and a frog gave you a bag of gold, how would you spend it? On your own or with a friend make a "witch wish list".

4. On your own or with a friend make a list of other books that Angela might have in her tower library.

5. Read *The Witch's Handbook* by Malcolm Bird (St. Martin's).

6. For a different picture of witches read Roald Dahl's *The Witches* (Farrar).

7. Write the story of how Sam, the frog, came to have three bags of gold.

8. *Rumplestiltskin* is a folk tale that involves a person having to guess someone's name. There are many versions of this tale. Find one and share it with the class.

9. If Aubrey, Andrea and Angela had guessed Sam's name, and it turned out that he DIDN'T have the promised three bags of gold, what would the sisters have done? What would you have done in their place? Discuss.

10. Twins and triplets often have names that start with the same letter. As a class, make a list of twins you have known who have names that begin with the same letter or sound similar.

11. Learn the *Name Game* from Heather Bishop's recording *Purple People Eater* from Mother of Pearl Records Inc.

12. Why were you named what you were named? Share the story of your name with the class. What does you name mean?

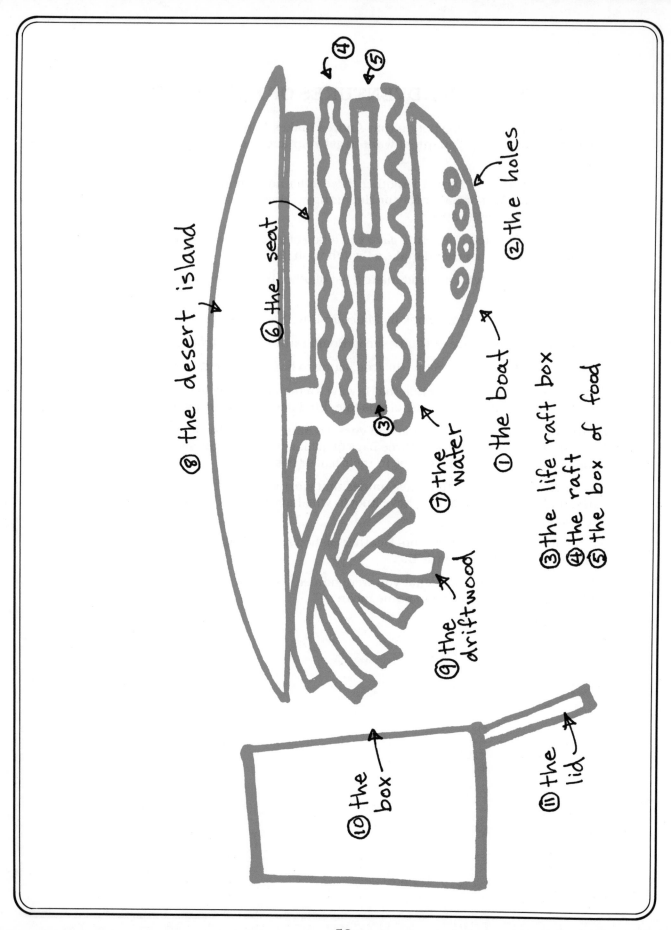

① the boat
② the holes
③ the life raft box
④ the raft
⑤ the box of food
⑥ the seat
⑦ the water
⑧ the desert island
⑨ the driftwood
⑩ the box
⑪ the lid

THE CASTAWAYS

NOTE: You will need to turn the drawing over at the end to see the finished picture. Do your drawing on a piece of paper on an easel or on a transparency on an overhead projector. Obviously, a blackboard won't work.

Danny bought a boat from Bob, and he invited Rick to come and have a ride. [*This is the boat.*]

They put on their life jackets and cast off. They sailed quite a long way from shore. Suddenly, Danny noticed that several small holes had appeared in the bottom of the boat and water was streaming in.

"There is a rubber raft in that box, Rick." he cried. "You pump it up while I try to bail."

Rick unpacked the life raft, but pump as he might, the life raft stayed as limp and as flat as a dead balloon. And no matter how fast Danny bailed, the water kept getting higher and higher.

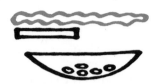

"It's no use!" yelled Danny. "We're going down."

He grabbed the box of food and threw it overboard.

They ripped out one of the seats to cling to, and just in time, because at that moment . . .

. . . water spilled over the gunwales and the boat sank out of sight.

Danny and Rick floated for a long time. Eventually . . .

. . . they spotted land and managed to paddle ashore.
"Castaway on a desert island!" moaned Danny. "We'll starve to death."

"How do you know this is a desert island?" said Rick.

"Of course it is!" said Danny. "We're shipwrecked aren't we? I wonder if the food box washed ashore?"

The two castaways looked up and down the beach. If the food box had been washed ashore, they couldn't see it.

"We're going to die!" wailed Danny. "We're going to die!"

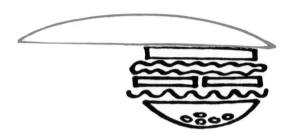

"Calm down," said Rick. "I'll go and explore and see if I can find us something to eat. You collect some driftwood to make a fire."

So Rick went off and Danny set to work collecting driftwood and putting it into a pile. The whole time he worked, Danny got hungrier and hungrier. And the whole time he worked, Danny worried.

"What if he can't find anything . . . What if he catches a rabbit . . . I can't skin a rabbit, and it would taste yukky with the skin on . . . What if something eats HIM instead . . . What if he captures a monkey . . . I couldn't eat a cute little monkey . . ."

And he was still worrying when . . .

. . . Rick came back carrying a cardboard box.
"What do you have there?" Danny asked.
Rick opened the lid and, when Danny saw what was inside . . .

. . . he FLIPPED.

TURN THE
DRAWING
AROUND...

"How did you find hamburgers, french fries and a milkshake on a desert island?" he cried.
"This isn't a desert island, Danny," said Rick, shaking his head. "There's a shopping mall right behind those trees."
But Danny was already busy eating . . .

TELLING POINTS

1. Because you must turn the image around at the end, you must do this story on a sheet of paper—a blackboard won't work.

THE FURTHER ADVENTURES OF THE CASTAWAYS

1. Read *The Swiss Family Robinson* by Johann David Wyss (Buccaneer Books) or *Swallows and Amazons* by Arthur Ransome (Jonathan Cape Ltd.).

2. Make a map showing where the castaways sailed, how far they drifted and where they came ashore.

3. You are walking along the beach and you see boxes, a deflated life raft and other debris washed up on the sand. What do you do? Discuss.

4. Read *Nicole's Boat* by Alan Morgan (Annick Press).

5. If you were marooned on a desert island—assume you have food, shelter and clothing—what three things would you wish to have with you? Share your choices with the class and discuss.

6. If you were Danny and someone sold you a leaky boat, what would you do? Discuss. Have a friend take the role of the person who sold you the boat. Act out the meeting you have when you return from your adventure.

7. Tell the story in the first person—as if it really happened to you. "One day my friend came and told me he'd just bought a boat . . ." or "I bought a boat and I said to my friend . . ."

8. Danny is worried about what Rick is going to bring back for him to cook. Make a list of things you think Danny might have come back with if the island had really been a desert island.

9. Do some research and make a report to the class on boating safety.

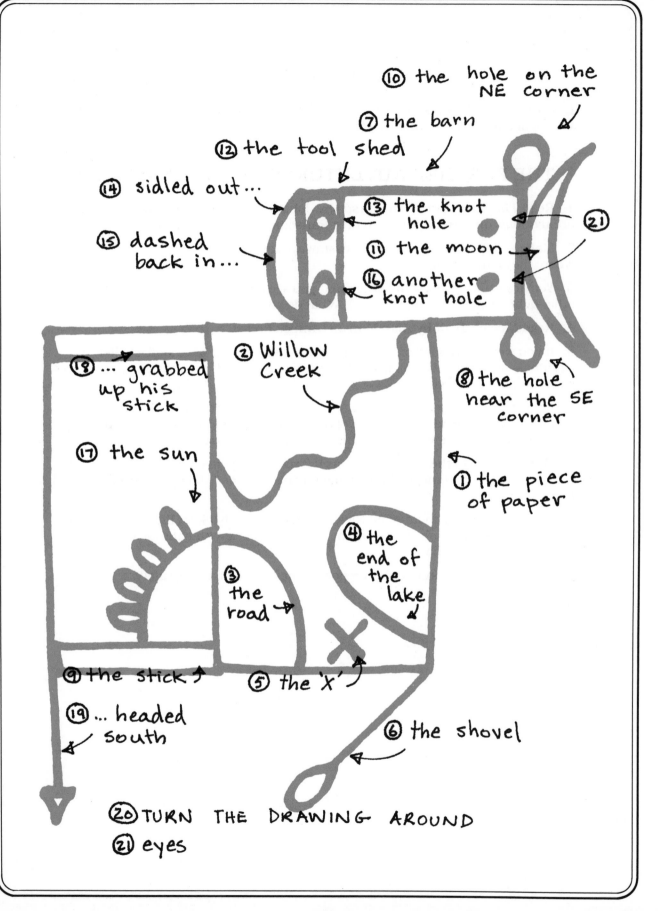

⑩ the hole on the NE corner

⑦ the barn

⑫ the tool shed

⑬ the knot hole

⑭ sidled out...

⑮ dashed back in...

⑪ the moon

⑯ another knot hole

㉑

⑱ ...grabbed up his stick

② Willow Creek

⑧ the hole near the SE corner

⑰ the sun

① the piece of paper

④ the end of the lake

③ the road

⑨ the stick

⑤ the 'X'

⑥ the shovel

⑲ ... headed south

⑳ TURN THE DRAWING AROUND

㉑ eyes

THE GHOST ON PEDERSEN'S FARM

NOTE: You will need to turn the drawing over at the end to see the finished picture. Do your drawing on a piece of paper on an easel or on a transparency on an overhead projector. Obviously, a blackboard won't work.

Gordie couldn't believe his luck! He'd just been thumbing through the Farmer's Almanac and out dropped this piece of paper.

As soon as he'd got a look at it, Gordie knew what it was . . .

There was Willow Creek, and the piece of the road that ran by Cranberry Hill, and there was a bit of the west end of Badger Lake. And down in the corner was a black 'X'. It had to be a treasure map! And that 'X' was right where Holgar Pedersen's Farm used to be. Old Holgar must have buried his money there, made this map, hid it in the book, and then he up and died before he could tell anybody about it. So nobody knew about the treasure out there on Pedersen's farm . . . except Gordie!

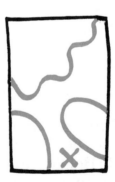

That same night, Gordie took a shovel and went out to the abandoned farm. It was dark that night—darker than a blind rat in a root cellar. But Gordie was happy about that, because nobody was likely to see what he was up to.

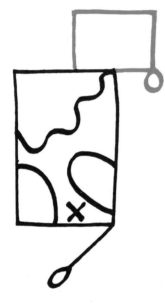

He decided to start looking out by the barn. He took off his coat and he started to dig a hole, [*right here*] near the south east corner.

He'd been working a while when he heard a mournful moaning and groaning sound— "OOOOOoooo!" He stopped digging and listened. Nothing.

"Just my imagination," he said to himself.

A while later he heard it again— "OOOOoooo."

Well, that got Gordie thinking about all the stories he'd heard about how folks had seen Old Holgar's ghost out on the farm some evenings doing the chores.

"I'm not letting no ghost keep me from my treasure," he said to himself.

And he got out of the hole and got himself a big stick. He shook the stick at the dark, and he hollered out: "Listen to me, ghost. You come moaning around here, I'm gonna whop you with this stick!"

And he went back to digging.

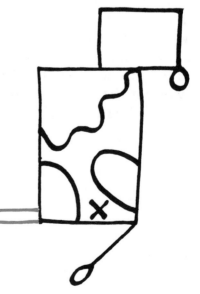

Well, Gordie was down about a metre and a half on the south east hole when he decided that that couldn't be the right spot. He moved over and started digging on the north east corner.

He'd just started the new hole [*here*] when he heard it again, low and mournful—"OOOOOoooo."

He stopped. The noise stopped.

He started digging again. There it was again—"OOOOOoooo".

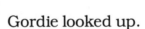

Gordie looked up.

Right then the clouds moved off and a crescent moon came peaking out. By the light of that thin moon, Gordie saw the dark shape of Holgar Pedersen's ghost coming toward him across the field.

"OOOOooooo"

Well, Gordie forgot all about whopping that ghost. He grabbed up his stick, and he ran straight into the tool shed [*here at the end of the barn*] and slammed the door behind himself.

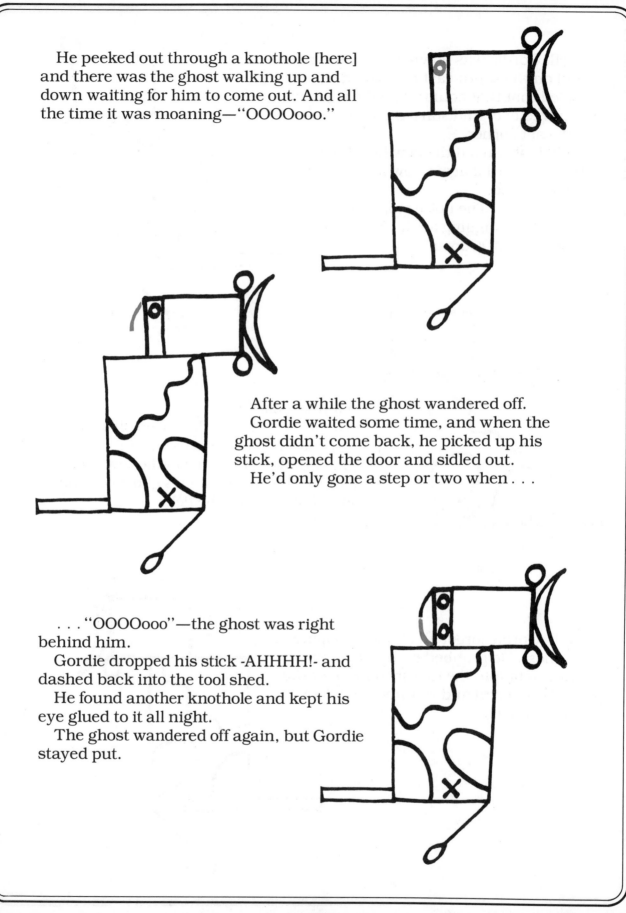

He peeked out through a knothole [here] and there was the ghost walking up and down waiting for him to come out. And all the time it was moaning—"OOOOooo."

After a while the ghost wandered off. Gordie waited some time, and when the ghost didn't come back, he picked up his stick, opened the door and sidled out.

He'd only gone a step or two when . . .

. . . "OOOOooo"—the ghost was right behind him.

Gordie dropped his stick -AHHHH!- and dashed back into the tool shed.

He found another knothole and kept his eye glued to it all night.

The ghost wandered off again, but Gordie stayed put.

Finally—finally!—the sun came poking up over the corner of the barn and only then did Gordie open the tool shed door and venture out.

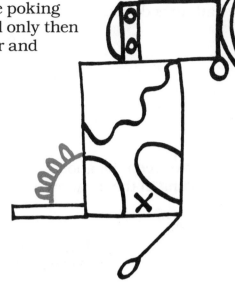

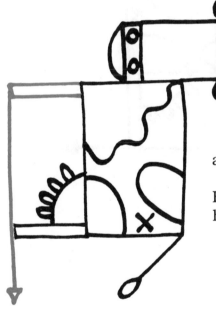

He grabbed his stick and headed south at a dead run.

He didn't turn around once to see if Holgar Pedersen's ghost was coming after him.

But if he had turned around . . .

TURN THE DRAWING AROUND...

He would have seen the ghost there alright—standing in the meadow, chewing on her cud.
"OOOOOoooo!"

TELLING POINTS

1. Because you must turn the image around at the end, you must do this story on a sheet of paper—a blackboard won't work.

2. Work on your "moaning and groaning". You want it to sound legitimately like a cow, but not too much like a definite "MOO". Quite often someone in your audience will guess that it is a cow just from the sound. If someone does, just press on . . .

3. Use a slow, quiet voice to describe Gordie creeping out of the tool shed. Then Gordie's yell—"AHHH!", when he hears the ghost, will be that much more effective.

THE FURTHER ADVENTURES OF THE GHOST

1. If you would like to learn some other spooky stories you might want to read *When The Lights Go Out* by Margaret Read MacDonald (H.W. Wilson).

2. Another spooky draw-and-tell story you could learn is *Cousin Vladimir* from *Draw-and-Tell* by Richard Thompson (Annick Press).

3. Read *Hidden Treasure* by Pamela Allan (G.P. Putnman) and *The Treasure* by Uri Shulevitz (Farrar). These two books raise some interesting questions about the nature of treasure.

4. Write a story about how Holgar Pedersen got a treasure and buried it. Where on the farm was it actually buried? Why is Holgar's ghost haunting the farm?

5. If the paper Gordie found *wasn't* a treasure map, what was it? And how did it get into the book? Write the real story behind the mysterious piece of paper in Gordie's book.

6. How would you define "being rich"? How much money would you need before you considered yourself rich? Discuss.

7. Write a story from the cow's point of view. Was she frightened when she heard strange noises on the farm? Did she think Gordie was Holgar's ghost? Was she trying to scare Gordie away, or was she just being friendly?

8. Did Gordie ever go back to the farm? Write the story of what happened to Gordie after his frightening encounter with the ghost.

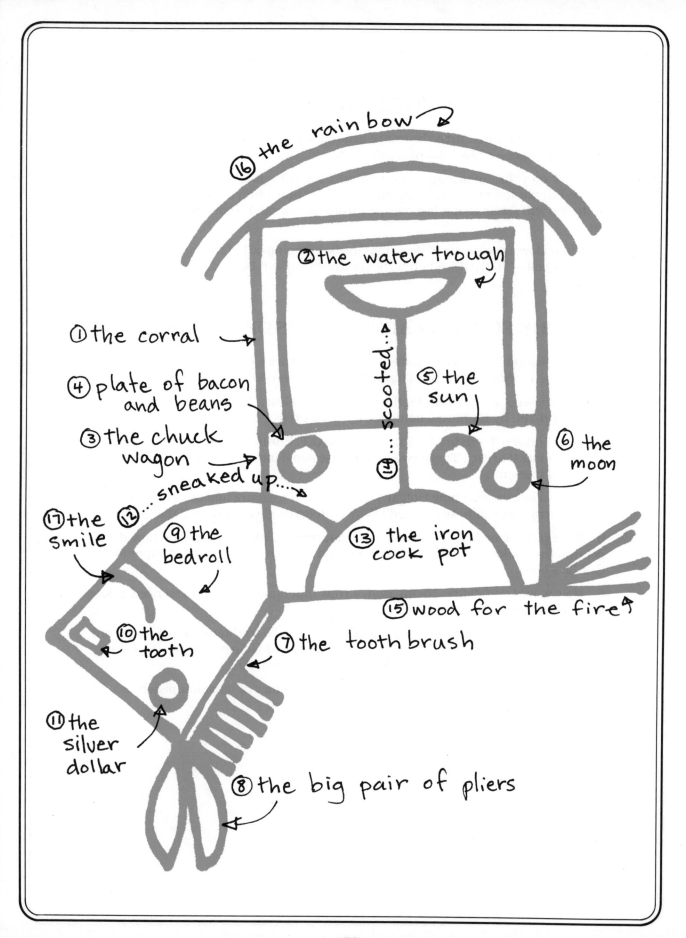

⑯ the rainbow

② the water trough

① the corral

④ plate of bacon and beans

③ the chuck wagon

⑤ the sun

⑥ the moon

... scooted ...

⑭

... sneaked up ...

⑰ the smile

⑫

⑨ the bedroll

⑬ the iron cook pot

⑩ the tooth

⑦ the tooth brush

⑮ wood for the fire

⑪ the silver dollar

⑧ the big pair of pliers

HANK AND THE TOOTH FAIRY

NOTE: You will need to turn the drawing over at the end to see the finished picture. Do your drawing on a piece of paper on an easel or on a transparency on an overhead projector. Obviously, a blackboard won't work.

Hank and Midnight came in off the range after a hard day of herding cows. Hank led Midnight into the corral. [*Right here.*] He took off the old cow pony's saddle and bridle and got him settled down for the night.

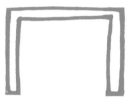

He filled the water trough up so Midnight would have plenty to drink.

He threw in a bundle of hay for his friend's supper.

And once his horse was fed and happy, Hank mosied over to the chuck wagon to see what he could do about filling his own belly.

He got himself a big plate of bacon and beans and settled himself down by the fire. He ate his bacon and beans. He sang some cowboy songs with the other cowboys. He told some cowboy stories and played his harmonica a spell.

The sun went down, and the moon came up, and by and by it was time for bed.

Hank got out his toothbrush and commenced scrubbing his teeth.

All of a sudden—"Yeowwww!"—one of his teeth started paining him something fearful.

He skedaddled over to the chuck wagon to see if the cook had something that might ease the pain a bit.

The cook took one look at the tooth and shook his head. "She'll have to come out, Hank. No saving her."

He got a big pair of pliers. He latched onto that tooth, and he pulled.

He pulled, and he wiggled, and he twisted, and pulled some more until, finally—POP!—out came the tooth.

"Well," said the cook, dropping the tooth into Hank's hand. "What you gonna do with this now? She ain't gonna be chewing no more steak, that's for sure."

Hank looked at the tooth. "I kinda thought I might put it under my bedroll. I used to do that when I was a young 'un, and I always got some money."

"Can't hurt to try," said the cook.

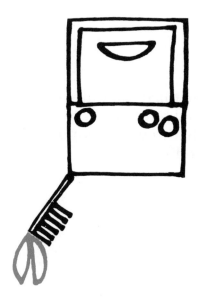

So when Hank rolled out his bedroll that night, he put the tooth under one corner [*right here*] and he went to sleep.

The first thing Hank did when he woke up in the morning—he felt under his bedroll. By gum, there was a shiny new dollar coin there.

"Hot dog!" said Hank. "That's more than I got when I was a kid. I guess they pay by weight."

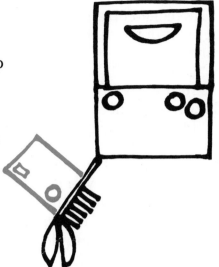

Hank got up, and he was starting to roll up his bedroll when he saw something moving over by the chuckwagon.

"Well, I'll be darned!"

There was the tooth fairy sitting there drinking a cup of coffee.

Hank sneaked up real quiet.

He picked up a big iron cooking pot and he set it down quick, right over the little mite.

"Gotcha!"

From inside the pot Hank could hear the fairy's tiny voice.

"Please let me go. Please, mister. There's boys and girls all over the world waiting for me to come and fetch their lost teeth."

"I'm gonna let you go," said Hank. "I just want to show you to the cook first . . ."

"No! No! You got to let me go now."

Well, the fairy sounded so sad that Hank just had to let her go.

"Sorry if I scared you at all," he said. "I didn't mean you no harm."

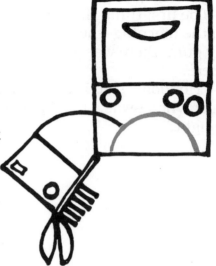

As soon as Hank lifted the pot, the tooth fairy scooted over beside the water trough.

She poked her little head out and she said, "Thank you for letting me go. And because you were kind, I will grant you one wish."

"Ah, heck," said Hank. "I don't need no wish."

"All the same," said the fairy. "The next time you see a rainbow, turn around once, turn around twice, and half again, and the thing you wish for shall be yours."

And then the fairy disappeared.

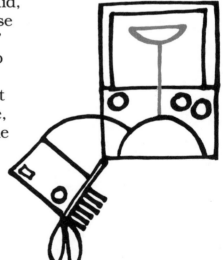

Hank went off to collect some wood for the fire, and didn't think much more about it.

Then he saddled up old Midnight, and the two of them headed out onto the range.

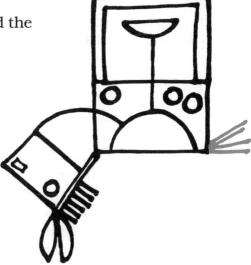

Now it just so happened that a huge thunder storm came rolling in that afternoon. There was thunder! There was lightening! And the rain just came pelting down!

But when the clouds rolled on, there over the hills Hank saw a beautiful rainbow.

Hank scratched his chin and he thought, "I can't think of nothing to wish for for myself, but Midnight—Midnight here is getting kind of old to be chasing after cows."

So he said out loud, "How's about I wish me a new horse."

He got down off Midnight, and he turned around once, and turned around twice, and half again.

There was a little dazzle of light just by a clump of cactus. Hank looked over . . .

TURN THE DRAWING AROUND...

. . . and there was his new horse.

"That's a new horse alright," he said, "But it ain't exactly the kind I had in mind."

But he took that horse into town and gave it to his nephew. And you should have seen the smile on that boy's face when he saw *his* new horse.

TELLING POINTS

1. This is one of those stories where you turn the image over. Remember not to try it on a blackboard.

THE FURTHER ADVENTURES OF HANK AND THE TOOTH FAIRY

1. If the tooth fairy was to give you one wish, what would you wish for? Discuss. You aren't allowed to wish for more wishes, by the way.

2. Read *The Tooth Witch* by Nurit Karlin (Lippincott).

3. Suppose the tooth fairy had agreed to stay around and meet the cook. Report the conversation that she and Hank and the cook might have had as they sat around the fire drinking coffee.

4. Being a tooth fairy is probably a dangerous and demanding job. What particular problems and dangers would a tooth fairy in the "Old West" have faced? On your own or in a group make a list. Share your list with the class.

5. Learn a cowboy song and sing it (or play it on the harmonica) as part of the story.

6. Would a tooth fairy in the "Old West" have looked different from a modern tooth fairy? Draw a picture. Make a book of portraits of famous tooth fairies throughout history. What would a prehistoric tooth fairy have looked like? What about a tooth fairy of the future?

7. Try telling the story with a cowboy's drawl for Hank's part and a tooth fairy voice—what kind of voice would a tooth fairy have?

8. Tell the story as if you were Hank. You might want to start off by showing your audience a shiny new dollar coin and saying something like: "Let me tell you the story of how I came by this here shiny new dollar coin. You see, my old cow pony, Midnight, and me were out on the range . . ."

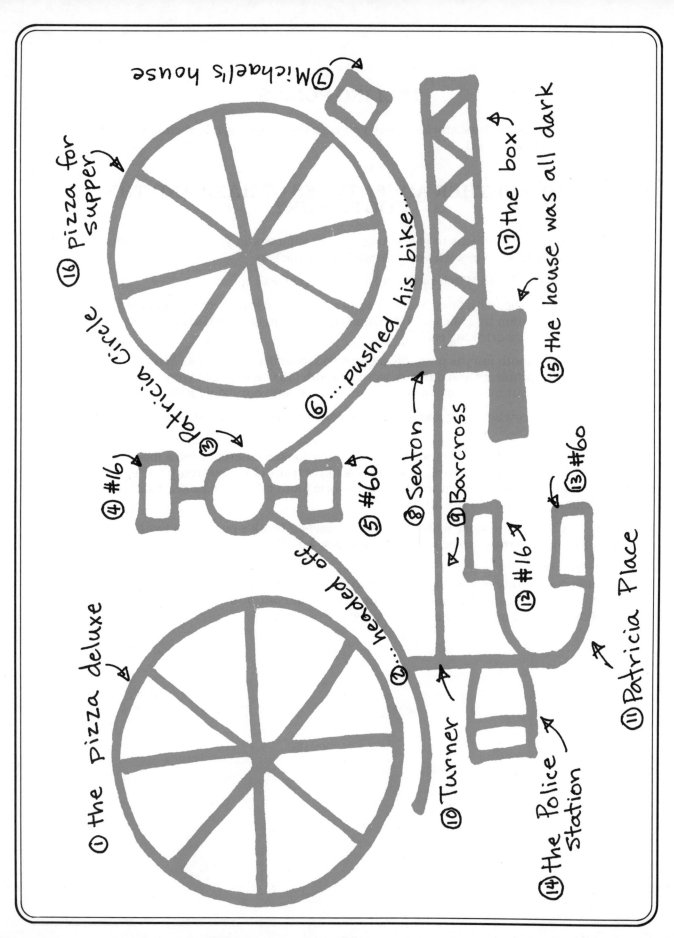

① the pizza deluxe

⑯ Pizza for supper

⑦ Michael's house

③ Patricia Circle

④ #16

⑤ #60

⑥ ...pushed his bike...

⑰ the box

⑮ the house was all dark

⑧ Seaton

⑨ Barcross

⑫ #16

⑬ #60

②...headed off

⑩ Turner

⑭ the Police Station

⑪ Patricia Place

THE PIZZA PEDALLER

NOTE: You will need to turn the drawing over at the end to see the finished picture. Do your drawing on a piece of paper on an easel or on a transparency on an overhead projector. Obviously, a blackboard won't work.

"Okay, Christopher, here you go—one pizza deluxe, everything on it, ready in the box piping hot! Take it to #16 Patricia. And then you can go home. No more deliveries today."

Christopher jumped on his bike and headed off down the street toward Patricia Circle. He'd be finished early, and that was good, because his mom had told him they were expecting company for dinner.

He arrived at Patricia Circle and rode up to the door of #16.

"There must be some mistake," the lady told him. "Maybe it was #60. That's around the other side of the circle. People often get mixed up."

Christopher rode around to #60 Patricia Circle. They didn't want the pizza either.

"Could it be Patricia Place you want?" the man at #60 suggested. "There's a Patricia Place right off Turner St."

When Christopher went back outside, his bike had a flat tire.

"Oh, great!" he muttered. "I'll have to push it home and get it pumped up. No wait! Michael borrowed my pump."

He pushed his bike as fast as he could down the street . . .

. . . to Michael's house.

While he and Michael were pumping up the tire, Michael's little sister came into the garage.

"You guys better hurry," she said, "or you'll miss the party."

Michael frowned at her. "Shhh!"

But Christopher didn't have time to worry about a party right then. He had to get that pizza to #16—or was it #60 on Patricia Place?

He jumped on his bike and rode away. He turned left on Seaton, right onto Barcross and left again onto Turner.

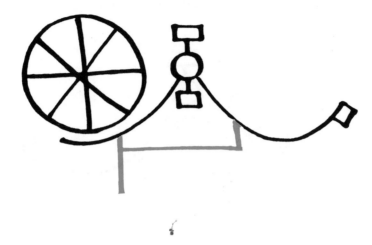

Finally, he arrived at #16 Patricia Place.

"We already had our supper," said the little girl who answered the door. "We had spaghetti."

It had to be #60.

Christopher rode around to #60.

"About time," the woman snapped. She opened the box and peered in. "It's stone cold," she declared. "I hope you don't expect me to pay for this!" And she shut the door.

Christopher turned around and—his bike was gone.

"What a disaster!" he moaned. "I got the wrong Patricia, I get a flat tire, my best friend is going to a party without me, I have to pay for a pizza deluxe out of my own pocket and now this! I'll have to stop at the Police Station and tell them about my stolen bike."

Luckily the Police Station was quite close by. [Right here on Lamplighter Drive.]

When Christopher finally got home the house was all dark.
"They've probably moved away and left me behind," he thought.
He unlocked the door and went in. As soon as he closed the door behind him, the lights came on.
"SURPRISE! SURPRISE! HAPPY BIRTHDAY!"

Well, it had been a rotten afternoon, but it was a great party. All his friends were there, and there was pizza for supper and a big cake.
And presents!

When all the other presents were opened, Christopher's father went out of the room and came in lugging a big box decorated with ribbons.

Christopher started to open the box, but his mother said, "You have it upside down, dear."

Christopher turned the box over, and took off all the wrapping. He opened the box and inside . . .

TURN THE
DRAWING
AROUND...

. . . was . . . A NEW BICYCLE!
It even had a special rack for carrying pizzas.

THE FURTHER ADVENTURES OF THE PIZZA PEDALLER

1. Retell the story using your friends' names and names of streets in your town. Look on a map of your town. Are there two streets, avenues, or crescents with the same or very similar names?

2. Write a description and/or draw a picture of the bicycle you would wish to get for your birthday.

3. Join a club or take a class to learn about bicycle safety and repair.

4. If you ordered a pizza to be delivered and it came late and cold would you pay for it? Discuss.

5. Have a POT LUCK PIZZA party. Have each person in the class bring an ingredient—grated cheese, tomato sauce, English muffins for bottoms, various kinds of toppings. Each person can assemble his or her own pizza.

6. Make an ICE CREAM PARTY PIZZA. Make the crust out of oatmeal cookie dough rolled flat on a pizza pan. Bake it. When it is cool, cover with a layer of softened vanilla ice cream. Freeze until the party, then top with peanuts, banana slices, sliced kiwi fruit, chocolate chips, shredded coconut etc. and drizzle with "tomato sauce" made out of strawberry syrup.

7. Do you know when the pizza was invented? What about the bicycle? See if you can find out.

8. Write a recipe for the world's yuckiest pizza.

9. What are some of the things you've done to earn money? As a class make a list. What are some other possibilities for jobs for kids in your community? Find out and add those things to your list.

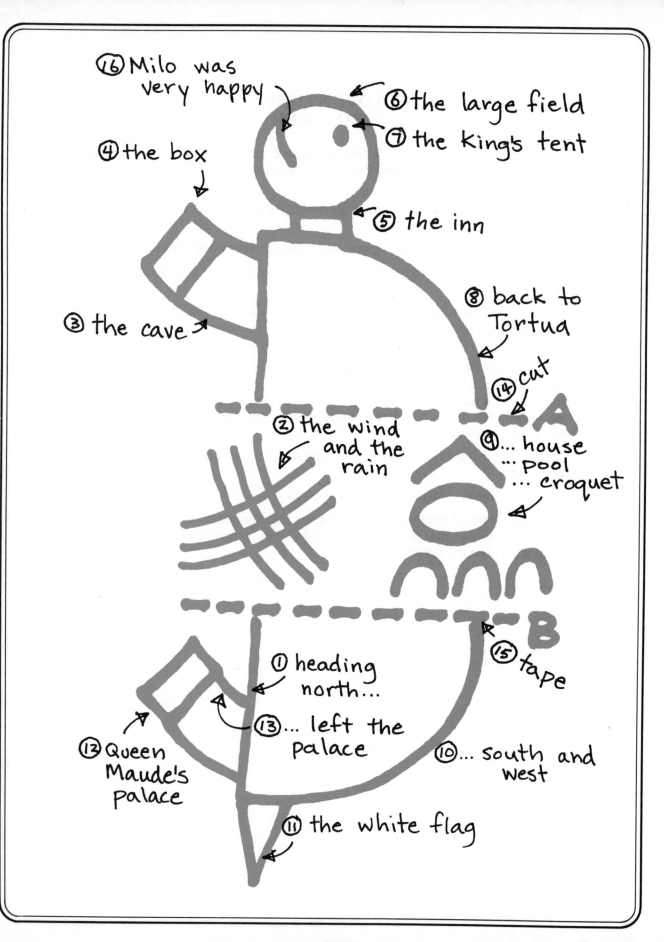

⑯ Milo was very happy

⑥ the large field
⑦ the king's tent

④ the box

⑤ the inn

③ the cave

⑧ back to Tortua

⑭ cut

A

⑨ ... house
... pool
... croquet

② the wind and the rain

B

⑮ tape

① heading north...

⑬ ... left the palace

⑫ Queen Maude's Palace

⑩ ... south and west

⑪ the white flag

THE WANDERER

NOTE: For this story you will need to cut the paper and tape it together for the final picture. Do your drawing on a piece of paper on an easel. Obviously, a blackboard won't work.

Milos was a wanderer. And usually he loved his wandering life.

But this particular day he was miserable. He was heading north along a deserted country road . . .

. . . the wind was blowing and a cold rain was pelting down.

Milos struggled on through the storm until he happened upon a cave.

Milos crawled into the cave, and was surprised to discover there . . .

. . .a small carved box.

Shivering in the darkness of the cave, the first thought that came to Milos was that the box might be traded for a hot meal and a bed if he could find an inn along the road.

He started out walking again taking the box with him, and by and by . . .

. . .came to a small inn.

He showed the box to the innkeeper and offered to trade it for a night's lodging and a meal.

"This box bears the Royal Seal," said the innkeeper. "Where did you get this, you scoundrel."

"I found it," said Milos.

"Found it or stole it," said the innkeeper. "Come with me."

Now, Harold, King of Tortua, had assembled an army to do battle with the army of his old enemy, Maude, Queen of Shelby. And, as luck would have it, Harold and his Royal Army were camped in a large field near the inn.

The innkeeper led Milos across the encampment to the king's tent.

Harold looked at the box and listened as Milos, shivering with cold and fear, told his story.

Then the king said, "This box belonged to my great grandfather. Legend has it that it was stolen from him by the great grandfather of the Queen of Shelby, and because of this box, our two kingdoms have been at war ever since. Now, my friend, it seems that the box was not stolen, but lost, and you have found it. Bring food and warm clothing for our friend! You shall return with me, Milos, to Tortua and be given a hero's welcome."

And the next morning Milos went with King Harold and all his army back to Tortua.

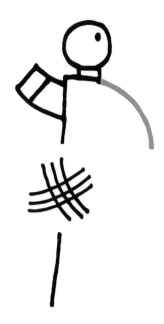

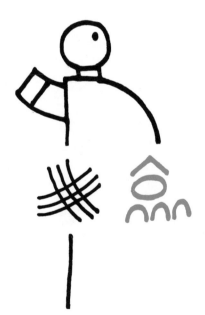

The king built a house for Milos, and every day Milos bathed in his private pool and played croquet on the lawn with the king and his family.

They had good food to eat. He was warm and dry.

But Milos was not completely happy. He yearned to be on the road again, seeing new sights, meeting new people.

So when King Harold came to him one day and asked him to accompany him on a mission of goodwill to visit Queen Maude of Shelby, Milos was delighted.

They headed south and then west toward
Queen Maude's palace. When they were
within sight of the palace, King Harold
ordered that a white flag be unfurled to
signal that they came in peace.

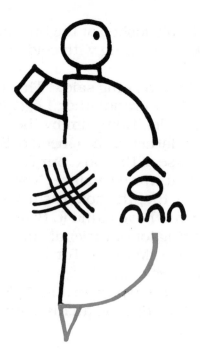

They proceeded to Queen Maude's palace
and spent a week there.

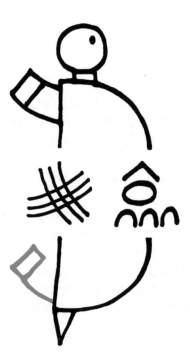

As they left the palace and came to the highroad north, Milos said to King Harold, "Your Majesty, I must leave you here. I am grateful for the friendship and for the house you have given me, but I am a wanderer, and the time has come for me to wander."

"But," protested the king, "when I met you, you were wet and cold and miserable."

"It is true that a wanderer's life can be hard," said Milos, "but it is the life that I would choose."

"So be it!" said the king. "But I cannot bear the thought of you cold and shivering in the weather. I have an idea. Will you come back to Tortua with me for one week? And then you may wander where you will."

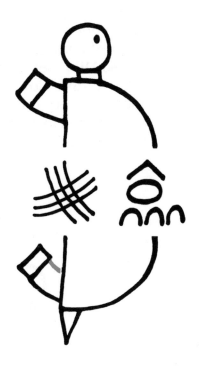

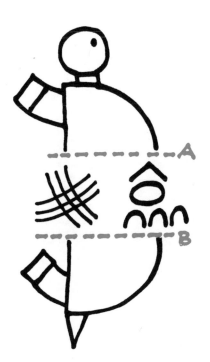

So Milos went back to Tortua with the king, and the king issued orders to his royal carpenters.

They hacked and tacked, they hewed and glued, they sliced and spliced, and finally it was ready. [*Cut the drawing at line "A". Place the "head end" to match the "tail end" at line "B" to hide the part of the drawing between the two lines. Tape in place.*]

"What is it?" asked Milos.

"It is a house that you can carry with you in your wanderings," declared the king.

And so Milos set off wandering with his new house on his back. He wandered more slowly, but more comfortably than he had before.

Milos was very happy with the new house. And ever since that day Milos' children and his children's children have carried their houses on their backs.

TELLING POINTS

1. For this story you will want to have a large pair of scissors and a couple of pieces of tape at hand.

2. DO NOT start the story by saying: "This is a story about . . .' You will either give away the ending by saying "a turtle" or lead your audience astray by referring to Milos as "a person".

3. If you are using chart paper to draw on, use the lined side. The lines will help you match the two halves of the drawing.

4. Practice cutting and fitting the drawing together again. I find it works best to cut the paper while it is hanging on the easel, and to take both pieces and fit them together on the floor or a table.

5. Keep the story going while you are doing your cutting and taping. If you need more time, add more details about the carpenters.

6. Note that the dotted lines "A" and "B" are not actually drawn on your figure. They are only there to indicate where you need to cut and tape.

THE FURTHER ADVENTURES OF THE WANDERER

1. Because the middle piece of the drawing disappears when you cut and piece the figure at the end, it really doesn't matter what you include in the middle portion. Add to and change the parts of the story and the drawing that are in that middle portion.

2. Why was the box so important? Make up a legend that shows why the box was so valuable that the families would fight over it for years.

3. Draw a picture of the box. What would the royal insignia of the King of Tortua look like?

4. The name of the two kingdoms gives a clue to the ending of the story— "Tortua" = tortoise and "Shelby" = shell. Think of some other turtle/tortoise puns and weave them into the story. For example, think of the name of the Inn or the innkeeper's name, the names of the King's children or the names of other royal personages Milos meets.

5. From where was Milos wandering? Where was he planning to go? Write several pages from Milos' travel diary.

6. Tortoise and turtle shells often have very beautiful designs. Do a drawing or a painting of the design you would put on your house if you were one of Milos' descendents.

7. Read *Franklin in the Dark* by Paulette Bourgeois (Kids Can Press).

8. There are many versions of the old tale, *The Tortoise and the Hare*. Find three examples and share them with the class.

9. Draw a plan of the interior of your ideal "wanderer's house".